THE CRYSTAL PALACE OF ADAMAS
Dedicated to: All the people of the planet Earth.
Richard M. Wainwright

Ron Walotsky

FAMILY LIFE
PUBLISHING

FAMILY LIFE PUBLISHING

Dennis, MA 02638 and Palm Coast, Florida 32135

Text Copyright © 1995 Richard M. Wainwright

Illustrations Copyright © 1995 Ron Walotsky

Graphics by Dan Dozier, Dozier Design

FIRST EDITION

Library of Congress Cataloging in Publication Data

Wainwright, Richard.:

The Crystal Palace of Adamas / written by Richard M. Wainwright;

illustrated by Ron Walotsky. -- 1st ed.

p. cm.

Summary: When Janus 777, a space pilot from an overpopulated highly technological planet, lands on Adamas, his life is changed by the friendly inhabitants and he must decide what to report home.

ISBN-0-9619566-8-2

[1. Science fiction.] I. Walotsky, Ron, ill. II. Title

PZ7. W1317Cr 1995

[Fic] -- dc20   94-16702

CIP

AC

The Crystal Palace of Adamas

Written by Richard M. Wainwright
Illustrated by Ron Walotsky

To *Elaine and Michael*

May your life and world be one
of peace, sharing and love.
Best Wishes,

*Best wishes for
wonderful lives!*

Ron Walotsky

Ron Walotsky

Richard M. Wainwright

Richard M. Wainwright

From *Mom and Dad with love!*

*Your friend,
Richard M. Wainwright
Merry Christmas
1955*

Gentle reader,

My name is Orrorak. My hair is silver; I am old but in good health. I have all my teeth and smile often. I am a member of the Council of the Chosen and its Chronicler. It is my responsibility to write the history of our small planet for all Adamians and their children's children's children.

Over one hundred and fifty years ago when I was born we had no Chronicler—we had no written language. Our known history was word-of-mouth tales from parents to children. This book relates important events in Adamas' history. I hope you will enjoy the story. Please remember that writing and this written language are new for me—new for everyone on Adamas. I will do my best.

With respect,

Orrorak, Chronicler

CHAPTER I

Janus 777 stretched, leaning back in the thickness of the pilot seat as his scout spaceship hurtled through the vast nothingness. His eyes mechanically scanned the inky blackness which was punctured here and there by distant stars. He had begun his odyssey from a mother spaceship located three light years from his home planet, Sagateum. Shifting his eyes to his instrument panel, Janus casually noted that his journey of 5 light years at timespeed (5 earth years) was almost over. Tomorrow he would enter a new galaxy designated G.600,555 on his universe chart to evaluate one of its small solar systems.

His orders were to explore, report and return. He wondered if his measuring instruments would tell him if one of the planets was safe to land on. This thought did not excite him for in truth, each second, minute, hour, day or year was the same for Janus. Like the automaton masses of his planet, he simply existed. Although 26 years old, every waking hour of his life had been spent learning facts and training for this one mission. The rulers of Sagateum had ordained his purpose in life before he was born.

Janus had been created, trained and some would say programmed, to be a galactic pilot. He could sleep for days, exercise only occasionally and still be fit, ingest sufficient nutrition through skin patches when asleep and eat food pellets when awake. Janus was never bored as he monitored flight instruments, recorded asteroid sightings and viewed technical video tapes which filled thousands of hours. His mind was like a sponge. What he saw or heard, he never forgot. When he didn't want to memorize, Janus turned off his mind and went to sleep.

Sagateum's ruling class, known as the Elite and led by the cruel Cagulus, believed their humanoid species was the most advanced in the Universe. Often they lived to be two hundred years old. After thousands of years their planet had become very crowded, but with the invention of intragalactic space ships everyone believed hundreds of virgin planets would be discovered. These planets would be suitable for colonization and be an unending source of natural resources. Much to the Elite's dismay, centuries went by and only one usable planet was found. Now Sagateum was over-populated and its resources depleted. Stern rulers governed the planet and based all their decisions on survival logic and technology. Human needs and emotions were never considered.

The Elite created Janus. Emotionally, he was like all Sagatiens—empty. He did not like or dislike any other member of his species. Words like love, compassion or even concern were not in his vocabulary or in Sagateum's lexicon.

The masses were awakened daily by sirens and trudged trance-like to assigned tasks in factories, offices or spaceports. Their pay—a weekly allowance of food pellets, a room in a monolithic apartment building and a television set with a single government channel.

Janus' life was quite different, yet his thoughts were more robotic than human. He had been genetically designed in a test tube and born to fill a specific societal role—space pilot. He had no mother—no father. He had only a vague rememberance of one woman named Mytius. Janus grew up under the care of a trained cadre of technical teachers who fed him massive amounts of information. They taught their space pilot children the complex skills needed to accomplish their pre-determined mission. All day, every day was spent learning and practicing. Once trained, young pilots were taken to motherships stationed in distant galaxies and sent on long search missions. Some perished in space but many returned years later to their mothership having failed to find a suitable planet for exploitation. The search for hospitable, resource-rich planets had become desperate and had been intensified. The survival of Sagateum's Elite ruling class depended upon new resources. No one and nothing else really mattered.

During his monthly transmissions to his mothership, Janus would visualize the thousands of towering gray skyscrapers beneath a plastic sky dome which completely enclosed Sagateum. Highways and sky paths weaved in and out between buildings. There was little open space and no live vegetation—trees and flowers were plastic. Over the centuries, the fields, forests and mountains had given way to apartments, office complexes and factories. No rivers or lakes survived. The few reservoirs were barricaded by high walls and guards. Water was rationed and recycled. Every drop was precious. Food was made synthetically in laboratory factories. The only animals to be seen were in history books and museums. There were no pets.

The busiest places on Sagateum were the scattered launching ports where space ships constantly departed and arrived. Shuttle flights carried men and women to nearby planets that were being mined, but they returned with barely enough mineral resources to sustain Sagateum's survival. Time was running out for the masses of Sagateum. The Elite, by the thousands, left daily for vacations in another galaxy which contained a solar system with one small hospitable planet. When first discovered, the planet had beautiful lakes, mountains, forests and animals. One of Sagateum's first galactic space pilots had discovered this planet. Tealius was his name and that was over one thousand years ago. Vacationers to this paradise honored its discoverer in every way possible. The planet was named Tealium. Statues, avenues and launching ports were named for Tealius. His early discovery of a pristine planet, soon after the beginning of intragalaxy space flights, encouraged the Elite Sagatiens to treat this beautiful planet no differently than when their own planet was young.

Millions of yearly visitors rapidly changed the face of Tealium. At first Sagateum's ruling class was not concerned with husbanding Tealium's resources or preserving its natural beauty. Huge resorts were built. Lakes became polluted or dried up, forests and animals disappeared and mountains were leveled. Too late, the rulers realized this paradise for the privileged would soon be only a wasteland. More Tealiums must be found. Janus was only one of hundreds of young space pilots streaking across the universe searching for them.

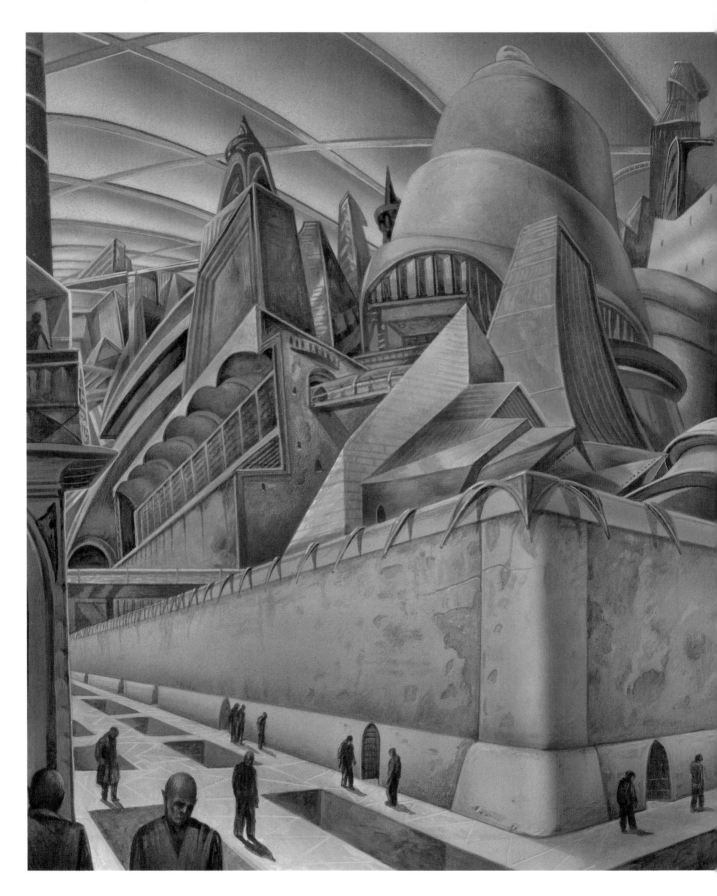

Janus earnestly studied his radar. The target solar system was materializing on his green screen. An averaged-sized star served as its sun. Four planets at various distances orbited the bright star. Using a computerized powerful telescope, Janus was quickly able to zoom in on one planet at a time. Not surprisingly, when he looked at the closest planet to the sun, he could see its surface was bubbling and explosions from volcanoes were shooting fiery molten magma and gases thousands of feet above its pulsing surface. It took only milliseconds for the computers and data analyzers to flash a warning message:

Planet I: Too hot for life for our species. Recommendation: Do not land.

He switched to planet number II. It was cloaked in massive swirling clouds. He waited for the computers to print an analysis. It wasn't long in coming:

Planet II: Surrounded by toxic gases. Landing and exploration require portable breathing system. Chances for any type of life almost zero. Harvesting of mineral resources would be extremely difficult. Recommendation: Do not land.

Planet III's orbit was considerably further away from its sun. Fluffy white clouds floated in a deep blue sky. The land beneath appeared to be shades of brown, green and blue with areas reflecting flashes of brilliantly colored light. It was a small planet compared to many in the universe.

Planet III: Initial analysis indicates a hospitable atmosphere, water and minerals. Three moons are orbiting this planet. Recommendation: Explore.

Janus felt a twinge of emotion. He would be landing on one of the planets. The discovery of a usable planet in this galaxy would guarantee him an exalted position among his planet's Elite hierarchy.

Planet IV's analysis was complete. The radar screen showed a dark grayish planet orbiting a vast distance from its sun. Deep craters could be seen clearly. It appeared devoid of any atmosphere.

Planet IV: Dead—no atmosphere. Possible source for minerals. Temperatures 200 degrees below zero. Recommendation: Exploration requires large expedition.

Two possibilities in one solar system. According to reports of thousands of space pilots, one possible planet to explore in a solar system was rare—two, unheard of. To date, no pilot had found a second livable planet—another Tealium. Janus punched landing instructions into his computer.

Reversing thrusters roared, Janus' spaceship began to rapidly decelerate into the planet's atmosphere. Long-range video cameras swept the terrain below searching for the safest landing site.

Landing sites selected. First choice: smooth mountain plateau. Second choice: desert area. Third choice: dense forest with small clearing. Will guide spacecraft to first choice unless pilot overrides system—now.

Janus didn't move, content to let the computers make the landing choice and guide him down. After five years in space and barring a catastrophic mistake by his computers, he would be taking his first steps onto a new world. His heart beat a little faster.

The flightdeck instruments showed that forward speed of the saucer-shaped spaceship had stopped. Telescopic landing pods extended and then locked in place. The spaceship ever so slowly began its vertical descent. Finally the feet of the three pods touched the earth, raising little puffs of dust as they settled firmly on the new planet. Janus smiled. He activated a powerful antenna. After it was deployed and oriented toward his mothership, he spoke slowly.

"Janus 777 has landed safely in solar system 600,555 on Planet III. Will report in directed time frame. End transmission. Janus 777."

Methodically, Janus began shutting down the many electronic systems used during flight and switched others to minimum power levels. Before lowering the doors and stairs, he adjusted his pre-packed exploration backpack and tested the readiness of a small but powerful ray gun. Janus was ready. The door silently opened and Janus walked down the stairs and stepped into a beautiful day.

The view was breathtaking. Above, cotton clouds lazily drifted across a powder blue sky. Behind him a mountain rose precipitously to a snow covered peak. At his feet crystals sparkled from partly exposed rocks. Below, a dark green forest gently descended until it reached the valley floor divided by a serpentine river. Janus stared. He turned in circles to enjoy the magnificent vista, snapping mental pictures.

Finished, Janus moved to the edge of the mountain plateau and took his first step toward the distant valley. He was still above the tree line and noticed rocks with algae and lichens. Soon he came to emerald green mosses and scattered wildflowers. He picked one and sat on a stone to examine it. It smelled sweet. This was the first live plant he had seen outside of the horticultural laboratory on Sagateum. Its beauty was magical and generated a funny feeling—a nice one—one he had never experienced before.

Janus entered the shadowy multi-colored forest. Leisurely, he chose his way. He stopped often to admire the metallic like trees and vegetation. Some appeared to be similar to pictures he had seen in books but most were unknown to him. It was cool and beautiful in the shade of the trees as light filtered through large leaves spotlighting the shades of brown and green of the many different grasses and ground plants. Funny looking birds and animals watched him with curiosity but with no fear.

Suddenly Janus' peaceful world was shattered by unintelligible shouts and screams from unseen people. Although he couldn't understand the words, the fearful quality of the sounds was unmistakable. Impulsively, he began to run and drew his laser pistol. Emerging from the forest he found himself on one side of a flower-filled meadow dotted with a few trees. The sight he saw was not pretty. A few yards away,

a huge creature covered with flashing platelets, a monstrous head and a gaping jaw was rapidly overtaking two running people. Janus' first thought was simply to watch but a deeper instinct urged him to help. He began to run. He needed a clear shot. The woman tripped, fell and struggled in vain to get to her feet. The man, armed only with a spear, turned to face the charging, roaring beast.

It looked like Janus was going to be too late. The man courageously decided not to wait for death but dashed toward the monster. This unexpected reaction caught the beast off guard. It reared up on its hind feet giving the man the opportunity to thrust his spear into its soft underbelly. The beast roared in pain but the wound seemed only to enrage the animal whose fierce eyes swung wildly about searching for his attacker. Finding him, the creature whipped his long tail to the left, encircling the struggling man. The woman screamed, staring in horror as the beast began to lower his head toward its captured prey.

Janus froze. He had a clear shot. He raised his laser pistol and fired. The beast raised and turned its head in protest but the laser beam was merely refracted by the crystalline scales. Janus took careful aim at the creature's large glassy eye and pulled the trigger a second time. An agonizing bellow followed and the creature's tail uncoiled as the huge animal tottered and then slowly fell on its side. With a dying gasp it lay still. The man, dazed, forced himself to his feet and stared uncomprehendingly at Janus. The woman turned to follow the man's gaze. When she saw Janus, she acted shocked but not afraid. She held up a delicate hand and smiled. Janus returned her smile and holstered his pistol. The man shuffled slowly forward making sounds, smiling and holding out his two hands. He was about the same size as Janus but with brown hair. Janus had no hair. No one on Sagateum did and he wondered what these two thought of him.

The man stopped in front of Janus, took both of his hands and grinned. He repeated the same unintelligible sounds three times. As they walked toward the woman the man continued to speak. She was slightly smaller with long, golden brown hair which seemed to glow. Janus guessed that the man had introduced the woman. He heard the sounds "Torak" and "Loria" several times. The woman's lower leg was either badly sprained or broken. Janus quickly removed his backpack. Smiling, to reassure the man and woman, Janus sprayed a pain killer on the leg. Gently, Janus put an inflatable plastic splint around the leg to immobilize it. The woman and the man watched Janus closely, with interest but apparently unafraid.

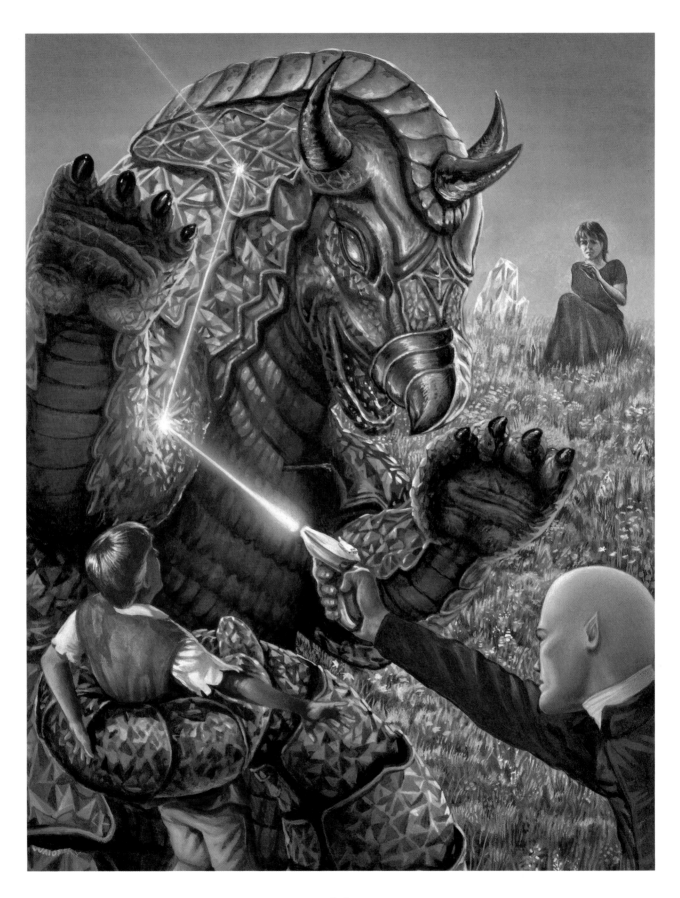

Janus was surprised at their reaction to him, considering his different physical appearance and high technology weapon. He expected these people would have been fearful or at least in awe finding an alien on their planet. Pointing to himself he repeated his name several times. "Janus, Janus, Janus."

Both nodded. The woman spoke first indicating she was "Loria." The man smiled repeating his name "Torak." Janus had guessed right.

Torak held up his hand indicating he wanted Janus to wait. He turned and walked to the edge of the forest. In a few minutes Torak returned with two poles and an armful of vines. Janus knew immediately what he planned to do and helped Torak tie and weave the vines to form a crude stretcher.

The men carefully helped Loria onto the stretcher. Janus shouldered his backpack and moved to the rear. Torak got in position at the front and nodded, then he and Janus lifted the stretcher in unison and began walking.

Janus laughed to himself. On Sagateum, no one bothered to help one another—the masses knew there were too many people. Few children were born. Lives were long. Each day was the same. People worked, returned to dormitory apartments, ate food pellets and spent the remainder of each day staring at a television screen.

Janus had been on this planet less than three hours and had changed. He felt strange emotions he didn't know he had. His orders were to simply observe, evaluate and report. Yet, he had reacted to the plight of fellow human beings. Janus felt needed and happy— emotions he had never before experienced. He was very glad he had intervened to save Loria and Torak. Some spirit deep within him had been awakened. He could feel some missing human feelings comfortably taking their rightful place in his soul.

These new feelings confused Janus, yet his years of training and indoctrination remained powerful. The purpose of his mission remained foremost in his mind.

Following a worn foot path, Torak carefully guided the trio through the mountain forest. Loria lay still. In less than two hours, they stepped into total sunlight. Nearby a clear mountain stream tumbled down the hillside toward the valley below. Janus thought it was the loveliest picture he had ever seen. And it wasn't in a book. Irrigation canals framed fields of yellows and greens. Like a checkerboard, a variety of crops covered the gently rolling hills. Janus assumed correctly: these people grew many different edible plants. A cold blue ribbon river flowed through the valley to a distant lake. Rainbow-colored buildings, clustered here and there, indicated a village.

On the other side of the valley cultivated hills gave way to a green forest beneath snowcapped mountains and volcanoes crowned by a shimmering spectrum of colors. Some crowns reflected blue light; others green, red, yellow and one a brilliant white aura.

As the land leveled, people came running and speaking to Loria and Torak; they asked questions and acted concerned. Most stared momentarily at Janus and then, as if remembering that it was not polite, returned their gaze to Torak or Loria. One young man ran off in the direction of the village. Janus noticed all the people were clean and neatly dressed like Torak and Loria. A small group of adults and youngsters followed them. Most of the people had light-colored skin and looked like Torak and Loria but several were quite different. These people were lighter or darker than Loria and Torak. A few were taller and their hair and facial structure distinctive. In less than half an hour the group reached the main cobblestone road of the village.

Stone houses bordered the road and each seemed to be surrounded by a soft glow of colored light. Janus had never even imagined such beauty.

A door was opened for them. They entered one of the homes. Inside a large room many people waited and gently removed Loria from the stretcher to a bed. First a woman gave Loria a large cup of a steaming hot liquid which smelled delicious while another woman examined Loria's right leg. She then opened a small box which contained many colored bottles. She dipped her hands in a basin of water beside her, opened one of the bottles and sprinkled some of the contents into her palm. After rubbing her hands together, she began, ever so gently, to massage Loria's leg. Janus could see by watching Loria's face that the pain of her injury was dissipating. Loria leaned against fluffy pillows, her face relaxed as the woman worked on her leg. Almost everyone had left the room and Torak motioned for Janus to follow.

Outside, Torak spoke as he patted Janus on the back. Of course, Janus didn't understand. Reaching in his backpack, Janus brought out a small silver box. It was a state-of-the-art language analyzer. Once the instrument understood the meaning of a small number of words of a language, it could translate hundreds more. Janus pointed to the building in front of them. Torak understood and repeated the word "tunton" several times. Next, Janus indicated a woman and then a man and heard "Adami and Adamo." In ten minutes Janus entered forty words into the computer and then it flashed, "Language analysis complete." Janus typed into the instrument, "Torak, my name is Janus and I live on Sagateum." The machine flashed back, "Torak, lu sum Janus do habum Sagetem." Janus then repeated the words out loud to Torak.

Torak smiled, nodded and simply said, "Tealax!" Janus' machine translated rapidly. "Bravo." Janus was surprised at Torak's mild reaction. He thought his powerful mini-computer would have stunned or at least amazed Torak with its ability to interpret his language so quickly. Funny, these people appear so simple, Janus thought, but are not awed by a foreigner with sophisticated technology. Strange!

Torak took Janus on a short tour of the village. He introduced him to everyone they met. All sincerely welcomed Janus, saying how much they admired his bravery and thanking him for saving the lives of their good friends, Loria and Torak. They did not gawk or appear surprised at his appearance as probably would have happened if an alien had landed on Sagateum. Inside one building, he met a friendly old man with silver hair by the name of Orrorak. He was using a crude printing press. He explained that writing was relatively new on Adamas. Nearby were younger men setting type. In another part of the building others were binding the pages together. Janus could see the paper was of a fine quality. On Sagateum paper was no longer available. In a third room women and men were sitting at tables writing, sketching or painting colorful illustrations for books.

As they continued their walk, Janus saw meticulously cared for fields and orchards. Torak described each plant and fruit and how long it took to grow. Most were eaten but a few plants were grown for ornamental, utilitarian or medicinal purposes.

In one of the fields a man guided a plow behind a strange looking animal. "That's a gannong," Torak explained, "it is our only large domesticated animal and it has a wonderful temperament. A gannong is very strong and with its six legs can pull the heaviest loads."

"Tell me about your irrigation system," Janus asked. "Your canals are superb and appear very effective."

"Yes," Torak responded. "Our stone builders, masons and the people who study our natural resources have worked hard over the years to give us a wonderful water system. We learn very young that water is indispensable for all life and we do everything we can to conserve, reuse and keep the water in our mountain reservoirs and rivers pure."

Janus asked many questions and smiled inwardly as he watched the people laboring with rudimentary tools. The hoes, rakes and shovels were made of brilliant stones and metals yet did not appear to be heavy. Younger people carried produce in woven baskets on their backs to waiting wagons while a few of the elders used sparkling wheelbarrows. Every person looked healthy and happy. Men and women sang and talked to each other while they worked. Dividing the fields were rows of fruit trees bearing all shapes and sizes of colorful fruit. People began leaving the fields. The planet's sun was approaching the horizon.

Reentering the house where they had taken Loria, Torak turned to Janus, "Welcome to our home. Loria and I will be forever grateful to you for saving our lives. Consider yourself a member of our family. Please follow me. I want you to meet all of your new family. It is almost time for us to sit down for dinner."

They entered a large room with many people. One-by-one, Torak presented Janus to his great-grandparents, Korak and Lia, his grandparents, Chorax and Teaia, his mother and father, Allak and Malia and his children, Starak and Sealia.

All shook Janus' hands and then hugged him. His rescue of Torak and Loria had created an instant bond. For the first time in his life Janus experienced a feeling that people deeply cared for him. He couldn't find a word for this feeling but it made him feel good.

Torak gently led a taller, hesitant boy by the hand toward Janus. "This is our son, Robak," Torak explained. "He is special to all of us and is a wonderful help to our family. Robak loves to work in our gardens and I think plants grow better when Robak cares for them." Robak grinned broadly and stretched out his hands for Janus to shake.

Janus warmly shook Robak's hands. He could see that Robak's head was different from the other children's, his movements slower and words fewer.

As Janus admired the long, polished crystal table set with lovely matched plates, dishes and sparkling blue glasses, the conversation hushed. Loria, her mother and father and children then re-entered, carrying trays of steaming food. Loria smiled at Janus and asked all to please sit down. Janus lowered himself onto a handsome stone chair. Thoughts darted through his mind. How had Loria recovered so quickly? How much did these simple people know about medicine and how did they create such magnificent homes and furnishings? Where had they learned to grow such a wide variety of plants? He had much to discover before he reported to his mothership.

It was the finest, most delicious meal Janus had ever eaten. Each vegetable was flavorful and had a wonderful aroma. He complimented Loria on the food, asking about each variety and how it was cooked. Loria was happy to tell Janus a little about each dish and about some of the herbs and spices grown on Adamas.

During the dinner conversation, Janus learned that the animal he had killed was a Creega. Creegas were the only known carnivores on Adamas. One had never been seen on this side of the Crystal Mountains. Stone cutters who ventured far to gather special rocks and crystals had reported on rare occasions seeing a Creega near the peaks but never in the forests. All the other wild animals on Adamas were herbivores and shied away from people.

Janus questioned Torak's daughter, "Can you tell me about the other animals you have on the planet?"

Sealia beamed and began to describe every creature she knew, from the large edible insects called axetels, to the rare poisonous snakes and toads named Sivas and Tovas. Hardly taking a breath, she described Adamas' fish, including the beautiful and delicious rainbow Cax and then its low woodland animals: the Dowie, Elton and Moosaw. Starak excused himself and quietly left the room.

"We have a few domesticated animals and beautiful birds," Sealia continued. Picas laid the eggs we ate and we have a pet Pugga. I think Starak has gone to get Loopi. Robak and I will bring in Puss. Sealia took her older brother's hand and disappeared.

Much to everyone's delight, Starak led their Pugga into the dining room for everyone to greet. Janus thought he had never seen such a strange, funny looking, large, colorful and friendly animal. Rainbow dots covered its body, six legs, four arms and long tail. It had tiny ears, a roundish head and an impish face. It, obviously, enjoyed fruit as Starak's grandmother handed the Pugga a reddish melon. It didn't eat it but held it in all four hands as a precious treasure to be savored later. After circling the table, Starak led Loopi out.

A minute later, Janus had his second surprise. Sealia and Robak returned sitting on the back of a very large, purring, gray and white animal. The huge cat-like beast gently sniffed Janus. At Sealia's insistence Janus, a little reluctantly, patted the massive head staring at him at eye level.

Torak reassured Janus that Puss was possibly the gentlest animal on Adamas. Robak had wrapped his arms around the massive neck of Puss and he rested between Puss' ears. Sealia climbed down and led Puss to a corner where she and Robak continued to play with their pet.

Naturally, Torak's family wanted to know about Janus' planet. He answered their questions truthfully but not completely. He described Sagateum, its bursting population and crowded cities, but did not mention the purpose of his mission or indicate what the leaders of Sagateum would do when he reported the beauty of Adamas. Except for that one painful thought, it was a long, enjoyable evening for Janus. When Torak and Loria guided him to his own room, Janus was ready for sleep. Tomorrow, his first full day on this beautiful planet, would be busy. He had much more to learn.

CHAPTER II

At first Janus thought he was dreaming. The sounds of tinkling bells floated across the room as he opened his eyes. Sunlight was directed against the rear stone wall creating a lovely rainbow of pastel colors. Aromas from something good cooking removed any doubts that he was awake. It was time to get up. He dressed quickly, washed and walked toward the dining room.

Loria and Torak were sitting, eating and talking. Both rose as Janus entered, welcoming him by shaking both hands and asking him to join them. Delicious looking breads, fruits and other unknown foods covered the table. Loria described every item before Janus began to eat.

"Janus," Torak began, "would you like to see what a typical day is for us? We would be happy to have you join us. In the morning our family will be taking care of our fields. Our days are long, with fifteen hours of sunlight. We have six days in our weeks and there are sixty weeks in our calendar year and I am sure you have seen our three moons."

Janus indicated he would enjoy being part of the family's plans. Loria passed him a second piece of the delectable bread and more of the luscious fruit marmalade.

"Can you tell me a little of the history of this planet and your people?" Janus asked.

Loria spoke up. "People, like us, have been on this planet for aeons. Our ancestors lived pretty much as we do today. We have added a few new things to our daily lives. For example, we use fire holders rather than fire stones and we have the wheel."

"Unfortunately, our forefathers did not have a written language so we lost much of their history. However, from stories and traditions that were passed on from one generation to another we have learned a great deal of our past. It was only a hundred years ago we learned to write our own language and another. Reading and books are now an important part of our lives."

Janus smiled and nodded, "Although I haven't seen much of your world I didn't notice any large cities or population centers as I made my descent. Did I miss something?"

Loria smiled, "No, you didn't miss anything. We are a world of small villages and always will be. We learned from our fore-fathers that our planet has limited natural resources. We must protect them with our minds and all our might. Families are responsible for raising sufficient food for themselves, their grandparents and great-grandparents. Our population grows very slowly even though people live to be 120 years or more. Every Adamian appreciates the natural gifts of our world. Our wise ancestors preserved the quality of life we enjoy today. We must conserve it for our children and future generations."

Janus indicated he understood. He couldn't speak because he was stunned by Loria's simple yet profound words. It was hard to believe that everyone felt the same way but he had no reason to doubt Loria. The meal over, Loria, Torak and their children, who had quietly joined them, prepared to leave.

Torak passed out glittering rakes, hoes and shovels to his family. Wearing baskets on their backs, Loria and Janus led the way to a nearby field. The children weeded and picked vegetables. Torak began turning over plants and earth in a small area that had already been harvested. Loria started pruning nearby fruit trees and at the same time picked the ripe fruit. Janus helped Torak rake the old plants into a pile. The smell of freshly turned loam and blossoming vegetables was delightful. Loria began singing. Her family joined her. Other happy voices could be heard from nearby fields. Everyone worked steadily and hours flew by. Mid-morning, Loria's parents arrived with food and something to drink. They all sat under one of their fruit trees chatting and eating before returning to their labors.

Even in illustrated books, Janus had never seen such a serene pastoral setting. Janus stood and asked for the shovel. Each shovelful of earth he turned was enjoyable and for some reason made him feel, for at least the moment, he was an integral part of life on this small planet. He and Torak made steady progress and by noon they had prepared the area for another planting.

Returning to the house, Janus played with the children and then everyone enjoyed a light lunch. According to custom, there was a short rest after eating. "Adults often read or meditate," Loria commented.

Torak took Janus to the library to show him their growing collection of books. Janus read the titles. Half were in the Adamian language but many had strange and indecipherable letters which he guessed were titles:

White Fang, Jane Eyre, Mountains to Climb, Red Badge of Courage, Don Quixote, Plato, The Pearl. Another language? Janus pondered. Then he skimmed through a book of *Adamian Traditions* while Torak read a book entitled *Democritus*.

Later Torak closed his book and looked up. "Janus, I'm sure you noticed our Robak is different. Very rarely on Adamas is a child like Robak born. Although he will grow physically, he will remain a child in most ways. We consider Robak to be a special gift to our family.

"This afternoon the children will remain at home to study and play while Loria and I go in different directions. Loria is studying stone and crystal cutting. Today I shall work with Orrorak at the printing complex. Why don't you go first with Loria and then stop by and see me?"

Torak and Janus replaced the books on the shelves and went looking for Loria.

As Loria and Janus walked through the village, she spoke of their neighbors. Loria explained that every family spent part of each day raising their own food and maintaining the beautiful canals and fish ponds. The remainder of the day people use their time pursuing personal interests like basket weaving, shoe making, glass blowing, growing and studying plants or fishing. "Some people raise bees for honey and create beeswax candles, others weave and make clothing, and artists paint or sculpt. Lots of people work on projects with the Natural Gifts Institute while others study at the Crystal Palace. In the evenings most families read, write and play together."

As they approached the outskirts of the village, a young man wearing a knapsack slowly jogged by. "Where's he going?" Janus asked.

"On Adamas villages are scattered all over our small planet," Loria explained. "Each one is governed by a Council of the Chosen. Communication between friends, families or the Council is done by messengers. You will see many messengers entering and leaving our village as the Crystal Palace is close by. Men and women arrange their schedules so they can serve as couriers one day a month."

"What a primitive system," Janus thought, "yet these people are very intelligent and obviously capable of creating wonderful and beautiful things. Why such a simple life?"

Loria continued, "You'll notice later in the day that many young people and adults are involved in sports which take place before the evening meal. On our weekly Day of Thanks, we often hike in the forests, visit nearby lakes and climb the smaller mountains. Yesterday when you saved us from the Creega, Torak and I had hiked to a lovely mountain waterfall and had spent several hours simply admiring the beauty around and below us. It was our wedding anniversary and we left the children behind with their grandparents. I'm very glad we did."

Janus smiled and nodded. Loria turned off the main road and followed a path through a wooded area. In a few minutes they came to a broad meadow. In the center a large, attractive, one-floor rambling stone building glittered in the sun. On both sides of the structure were piles of different colored stones—some large, some small. "Welcome," Loria said, "to our village's center for learning stone construction and stone and crystal cutting. Here, we also make glass. Masters teach. I have been studying ten years but consider myself just a beginner. There is so much to learn."

The heavy stone door swung open at Loria's touch and they entered together. Loria introduced Janus to each person they met in the corridor. "My study-work area is in the next room."

Men and women were working on stone tables and sitting on intricate stone chairs. One could easily see each handsome piece was different in some way. Loria noticed Janus' quizzical look and guessed what he was thinking.

"Yes, Janus," she began, "every person in this room made his or her own table and chair before learning to cut crystals. My table is this way."

Loria found an extra chair for Janus. On her table was a rock the size of a small melon. She picked it up and spoke, "We find these special stones close to the top of our volcanoes. Several times a year stonecutters and volunteers bring down baskets full of these beautiful stones. It is a dangerous expedition. There is always the possibility of an avalanche or a volcanic eruption."

"Inside the stones are magnificent crystals. I am learning to cut them in a way that brings out their beauty and creates usable shapes. Some crystals are harder and more difficult to work with than others. This one is an Adas stone, the hardest crystal on our planet. When cut correctly, its facets give off a brilliant bluish white light."

Loria picked up several large crystals pointing out cleavages in each where she would begin cutting by using small tools and oils mixed with Adas powder. It was slow work and Loria suggested Janus wander around and see what others were doing. "Don't worry. Everyone in this village knows who you are and what you did. You will be welcomed!" she said smiling.

Janus noticed that Loria's tools were metal. "This planet has minerals," he thought and somewhere there is a foundry." Slowly he walked around the other tables observing the care the artisans took cutting the colorful crystals. Many pieces were almost finished. He could easily see how the cut facets of the stones brilliantly reflected light. He greeted each person. All appeared delighted to meet him. Janus always thanked the artisan before moving on. In other rooms he met men and women mixing lime and clay which would become the mortar used to hold stones and crystals together.

Quietly opening another door, he observed a Master who was demonstrating cutting techniques. Through a window he saw large kilns where people fired the decorative and useful pieces made from clay, glass, stones and crystals. Janus was fascinated. Here was a simple society with a great deal of knowledge and expertise using basic tools.

Janus returned to Loria's side. He thanked her for sharing this part of her life with him. "Everyone here does beautiful work," Janus observed. "I would love to join a collecting expedition during my visit, if you think that would be possible," he ventured.

"You're in luck," Loria replied. "In a few days our village's stone masters will lead a group of volunteers to Danga—a volcano that creates our Adas stones. Torak will be going too and I know everyone would be pleased if you came."

Janus smiled and left to find Torak. As he wandered back toward the village, his senses were overwhelmed by the natural beauty of Adamas both near and far. Colorful wild flowers edged the twinkling gravel road and canals. Multi-hued fields and green forests led his eyes to the snowcapped mountain peaks and the glittering rims of Adamas' volcanoes. Janus wondered, not seriously, if he were dreaming.

"Maybe I'm still asleep aboard my spaceship," he said out loud. Feeling rather silly, he picked up a sparkling yellow pebble from the road and held it against his cheek. It was cool on his skin and very hard. For the first time in his life, Janus chuckled out loud. "I'm not dreaming," he thought and let his eyes return to the lovely world that surrounded him.

The printing building was easy to find. As he entered, he recognized Orrorak, who was talking with a young woman. Janus did not wish to interrupt them and started to quietly walk by, simply nodding and smiling.

"Please stop for moment, Janus," Orrorak requested. "I want you to meet someone. This is my precious and beautiful great-granddaughter, Sulia. She is the director of our regional Natural Gifts Institute. And may I say, not because she is my granddaughter, Sulia is one of the brightest young people on Adamas—one of our planet's jewels." Orrorak smiled and Sulia blushed.

Janus was almost speechless as he beheld the beauty of this woman. He could barely smile and hold out both his hands in greeting. Unlike most Adamians, Sulia had radiant black hair that covered her forehead and fell to her shoulders. Her complexion was a soft brown and her large sparkling blue eyes were highlighted with long black eyelashes.

"You'll have to excuse Papa Orrorak's tendency to exaggerate," Sulia responded with a warm smile. "I am very happy to meet you, Janus. I have heard of your bravery. Please accept my deepest thanks for saving Loria and Torak. You will always be welcome on Adamas. What have you seen and done so far today?"

"Please excuse me," interrupted Orrorak. "I have a meeting with Torak. I will see you later, Janus. Sulia, give my love to your family. Hope to see you again soon." He shook both of Sulia's hands, kissed her on the forehead and departed.

Janus, unsettled by the beautiful young woman who stood beside him, groped for words. "Your grandfather, Orrorak, seems to be a very special man on Adamas," Janus continued smiling. "And, he doesn't exaggerate greatly." Janus' eyes twinkled and he grinned. "But, to answer your question, this morning I worked with Torak and his family in their fields and after lunch I watched Loria and others at the stone cutting building. They are wonderful artisans. I am amazed at what I have seen."

Sulia smiled. "Would you be interested in visiting our Natural Gifts Institute? It is a short walk from here. I would be happy to tell you what we do and show you around."

Janus couldn't think of anything he would rather do. He knew, at that moment, whatever those lovely eyes suggested he would do. Regaining his composure, he asked Sulia to wait a few a minutes so he could tell Torak his plans. She agreed and Janus went looking for Torak. It took him only a few minutes to find his friend who thought a trip with Sulia a good idea. He suggested Janus invite Sulia to have dinner with them. The men shook hands. Janus returned smiling.

Sulia explained that the main building of the Natural Gifts Institute was on the other side of the village where the forest began. It would be an hour's walk but Adamians considered this distance to be a very short stroll. Adamians walked everywhere.

In response to Janus' questions, Sulia told him of her life and about her parents—Mirak and Marsia. She was an only child but lived like all families on Adamas in a home which included a great-grandmother and grandparents as well as her mother and father.

Before she could walk, her parents carried her in a backpack on hikes and camping trips. Sulia's Dad was a master stone cutter. Her mother's love was wildflowers and she was considered a flower authority on Adamas. Sulia set a brisk pace. Janus understood why Adamians appeared to be so healthy.

"Of course," Sulia continued, "like all Adamians part of my day is spent tending our family's garden, but that still leaves me plenty of time for my work at the Natural Gifts Institute. We just entered the N.G.I. boundary. We have no fences, but from this point on all the plants and trees you see have been planted and are cared for by N.G.I. people. In this area there is every species of plant you will find on Adamas. All are useful but some can be dangerous as well. For example, see that tall bush with long red, pointed leaves and large white berries? The leaves and fruit are used with other plants to make a strong medicine; but if you ate just one of those berries, you probably would die. It is the most toxic plant on Adamas."

Janus studied the odd plant closely.

"You can touch it," Sulia said, "but you must wash your hands well before eating anything. Fortunately, we do not have many deadly plants like that one. Over the years we have learned that plants not only provide our food, but with their great medicinal qualities ensure our long lives. We still have much to learn about them.

"The Natural Gifts Institute is the guardian of our planet's water supply, animals, forests and minerals. Our forests provide the wood for boat building, wagons and many other things. Minerals are used by our fire makers, stone builders, crystal cutters and tool makers. Our primary responsibility is to inform the Council of the Chosen about the known quantities of all animal species, mineral deposits and plants on Adamas and make recommendations regarding proposed uses by anyone or any guild.

Here we have a small foundry to separate metals, refine and study them and make a limited number of needed tools."

"One question answered," Janus thought. "Tell me about your fire makers, Sulia."

"Certainly," Sulia answered. "Ages ago our ancestors discovered fire could be created by finding the right type of stones and hitting them together to make sparks. During the past one hundred years we learned that sulfur and phosphorous, when combined in the right proportions, will with friction and oxygen create fire. At first wood was used for fire sticks but too many trees were being used for that purpose. We then recommended our stonecutters create stone fire holders and they are now used instead of wood. Because we have limited quantities of all minerals, we limit mining. We know once our minerals are exhausted, they are gone forever. Soon solar power will supply all our cooking and heating needs."

Sulia continued to point out the different varieties of plants, bushes and trees. A few birds and animals appeared as they walked toward the N.G.I. building. Near the entrance, Sulia picked two pieces of reddish fruit from a dwarf tree. "Try one. This is a hybrid Ollo. You won't see it in any of our gardens. We believe it has a better flavor than its parents and we think insects will avoid it. Eventually, the Ollo may replace the Lowta and Sigo fruit trees which families grow today. Do you like it?"

"It's delicious," Janus replied as he gazed in admiration at the multi-storied wood and stone structure before him. The complex's design blended in with the natural beauty of the area. The centerpiece was surrounded by lovely fish ponds, complete with miniature waterfalls, water lilies and lovely flower gardens.

As they walked inside, Sulia described the work and studies underway in the building and asked Janus what department he would like to see first.

Janus suggested minerals.

Sulia took Janus to a room where a large map of the planet indicated all known mineral deposits on Adamas. She explained that people who were interested in natural resources spent much of their free time during the year with miners and stonecutters collecting specific minerals. They were also responsible for exploring new regions in hopes of finding previously unknown mineral deposits.

In a second room, Janus was shocked. Seated on benches were individuals apparently using high-powered, state-of-the-art microscopes and spectrophotometers. Sulia introduced Janus to people who seemed happy to meet him and took time to answer his questions. As always, Janus was sincerely interested not only in the factual information but also in the person speaking. He thanked each individual warmly and shook both their hands.

Janus' head was spinning. Adamians seemed to be simple, caring people, yet highly intelligent with sophisticated technology. They were, obviously, capable of creating large buildings and complex machines but chose not to do so. Why did they live this way? They were so different from the cold, calculating Elite teachers who had trained him on Sagateum. Janus wanted answers but was patient. He would wait. Eventually, he would learn the secret of these people.

In two hours they visited just a few of the Institute's departments. Janus thoroughly enjoyed his tour with Sulia. While they walked between rooms, he relayed Torak's invitation to Sulia to join Torak's family for dinner. Janus added, he hoped she would say yes. Sulia agreed immediately and told Janus she considered Torak's family to be her second home—Starak and Robak to be her younger brothers; Sealia, her sister. As they left the Institute for the village below, Janus knew it would be a wonderful evening.

And, it was. Before dinner Janus and Sulia helped Sealia and Starak feed the family's Gannong and Loopi. Torak and Loria joined them to play one of the children's favorite games with a sponge-like ball. It was a lot of fun and many laughs; finally the sun called a halt to the game by disappearing behind the mountains. It was time to wash and prepare for supper.

The food was delicious and the conversation interesting. After dinner Loria strummed a stringed instrument and Torak played a flute. The children and Sulia danced and insisted Janus join in and learn the steps. For a moment Janus felt slightly uncomfortable with the wonderful feelings of family and friendship he was experiencing. He quickly learned the movements and then danced with everyone, including all the children, grandparents and Sulia. Time passed quickly with lots of laughter and applause. After the children went to bed, the adults sat in front of glowing crystals and chatted. Finally, Sulia admitted she was getting sleepy. Janus volunteered to escort her home. Torak and Loria smiled.

Sulia smiled, too. "Janus, it is perfectly safe for anyone to walk at night in the village," she remarked, "but I would be glad to have your company if you are not tired. I'd like to learn some words in your language."

CHAPTER III

Early the next morning, Janus awoke feeling rested and totally relaxed. Yesterday had been so wonderful. Slowly he reviewed all he had seen and done since landing on Adamas. His respect for the Adamians had grown tremendously. They were remarkable. Though they lacked Sagateum's scientific knowledge, their common sense and reverence for all life made them very special. A sudden thought jolted Janus like a lightening bolt. He wanted to stay. Sadly, Janus realized that in seven days he must transmit a report to the Elite waiting on his mothership and then begin his long return flight. He didn't feel as happy as when he first opened his eyes.

During the next few days Janus worked in the fields with the family in the mornings and spent the afternoons with Torak or visiting other artisans. Sarmak, one of the boat builders, invited Janus to go fishing. He took Janus out on the river. At

a bend, it widened into a small lake. After lowering the stone anchor, Sarmak explained the basics of fishing to Janus. Five times their conversation stopped abruptly as a large hungry rainbow Cax swallowed the bait.

Janus or Sarmak had to haul in the line as fast as possible to catch the fighting fish. Each fish was wrapped in a large green leaf to keep it fresh.

At sun disappearing time they pulled the boat out of the water. Sarmak insisted Janus take three of the fish. Janus smiled and said, "I'm sure Torak's family will love them but two would be plenty."

Sarmak also smiled, "Janus, I've enjoyed your company and hope we will fish together again. Possibly you may know of another family who would like a fish for dinner?" They shook hands and parted, Sarmak winked and grinned, "By the way, Sulia is my cousin."

Janus laughed, "There are few secrets in this village," he thought as he left for Sulia's house. Sulia and her family were very pleased to have the fish. They invited Janus to return another day. He was happy to accept their invitation before hurrying off to Torak's home.

Torak's family was delighted to have the large fish. Loria immediately passed them to her mother, Codia. Everyone in the household agreed Codia cooked Cax the best and left its preparation to her. Janus washed and joined the family. He was asked to tell of his fishing expedition with Sarmak. Later Torak described other species of fish that were plentiful in the mountain lakes as well as in the great blue waters.

Two more wonderful days passed for Janus and then it was the morning for the stonecutters' expedition to the high mountains tops. Loria, Torak and Janus met Sulia early at the village circle where they joined hundreds of other volunteers. There were at least a dozen wagons with teams of Gannongs in line ready to go. The director of the stonecutters guild stood on top of the first wagon and shouted words of welcome and thanked all for coming. Even though it would be hard work, today was a festive occasion. They all carried pack baskets of food, drink and extra clothing.

The wagons led the way; the throng followed. They quickly left the fields behind and climbed the foothills entering the forest. A well maintained, rutted track wound its way though the trees. Sun filtered through the branches, birds sang. It was a perfect day. People chatted as they walked and in a few hours the wagons reached the tree line. From there the going was slower as the Gannongs followed the rocky ridge toward the volcano.

Nearing the top, Janus could clearly see the jumbled ring of crystal shaped boulders and rocks which encircled the summit. Many looked like ordinary stones but others that had broken open reflected a glittering bluish white light. The carts halted a fair distance below the boulders. They could go no further. Torak led his wife, Sulia and Janus to an area nearby to empty their packs. With empty pack baskets they would climb to where the stonecutters were breaking up huge crystals and collect small pieces that were easy to carry.

The volunteers assembled and waited as the older stonecutters gazed at the mass of boulders above them. They alone determined where it was stable and safe to climb. Lives depended on their judgment. Janus stared at the jigsaw puzzle of shattered stones. He could not detect any rocks above that looked unstable but the stonecutters saw something and led the group away from the area to a new one. Again, they stood motionless, looking up and studying the mix of boulders and crystalline rocks. Finally they took two sharpened poles with red flags on the top and drove them into the ground.

The director stood on a boulder and shouted, "As you climb and collect stones, please stay within these two red flags. Keep looking back. We believe it is safe in this area but be careful."

Following Torak, Loria and Sulia, Janus began climbing toward the boulders above. The air was crisp and fresh. The climbers' movements were slow and deliberate. Loria found the first rock that was small enough to carry. It had broken off from a boulder and Loria showed Janus the beautiful exposed crystal structure. As they reached higher levels, more and more smaller pieces were easily found. Some had naturally split when they fell on other boulders during eruptions and others had been cracked by master stonecutters on a previous expedition. It didn't take long to fill baskets with the weight of enough stones to require the volunteers to carefully work their way down and carry their loads to the wagons. Each person made many trips. After several hours people began to stop and gather in small groups for lunch.

As they ate, everyone faced the valley far below just to enjoy the magnificent view. "Well, Janus, how do you like volunteer work?" Torak asked with a grin.

"It's really terrific," Janus answered "Cool pure air, a high altitude treasure hunt, great food and, of course, delightful company." He tried not to look directly at Sulia. "And, of course, a gorgeous view. What could be better? Tell me, do you have names for the mountains and lakes we can see?"

"Only a few," replied Loria, "To our left is Mt. George, Mt. Scott and Mt. Hakeem. On the right you can see Mt. Alexi and Mt. Jeremiah. The largest lake is Lake Jennifer and the four others you can see are Lakes Laura, Judith, Yoshiko and Carolyn."

Janus listened to the names—they didn't sound Adamian. He wondered why but didn't question Loria further.

While putting away the leftover food, Loria commented. "Janus, we will be leaving two hours before our sun disappears. If you hear a loud whistle, it means everyone is to return to the assembly area immediately." Janus nodded and with the others reslung his pack basket.

Up on the side of the volcano Janus lost track of time and did not pay attention to his exact location in relation to the red flags below. Without realizing it, Janus climbed outside the safe area. As he scanned the mountain side, he was struck by a blinding flash of light. He shaded his eyes and focused on a brilliant, bluish white, small, crystalline stone not twenty feet to his right. It was at the foot of several huge boulders. On top of the boulders a rock slab jutted out forming a shallow cave. He began to move in that direction. Halfway there he thought he felt a slight ground tremor. Seconds later, whistles began to blow and he knew he should start down, yet he was so close to the crystal. Seconds later, it was in his grasp.

Whistles continued to shrill. A second stronger tremor rippled down the side of the volcano. Large unstable boulders and rocks had been shaken loose and were bouncing down the mountain side directly at Janus. He looked above him in horror. Each boulder dislodged another and a full fledged avalanche was roaring his way. It was too late to run. He squeezed quickly between two boulders which supported a stone slab roof and waited hopelessly.

First a few small rocks hit the slab above his head and fell just beyond his feet. Larger stones and boulders immediately followed. The avalanche was deafening. Janus could see only a blur of dust, stones, crystals and boulders dropping in front of him and rapidly walling him in. The wall grew until Janus could no longer see light and the roar became muted. Thankfully, the overhanging rock slab above him held fast. Janus thought the avalanche would never stop. Yet in less than a minute it did. The silence, after so much noise, was equally scary. He wondered how thick was the prison wall that now entombed him. He listened but couldn't hear voices or whistles. He sat in blackness feeling very much alone.

Seemingly for hours Janus remained motionless listening for sounds. After many hours he realized the sun must have disappeared and the people forced to leave. No one could climb in the dark. Janus guessed the night would be cold but he was more concerned with air. He knew his supply of oxygen was limited and he needed to try to create at least a small opening. He carefully rose and gingerly began to feel for smaller stones near the top of the wall. When he discovered one, he felt all the others that surrounded it before he attempted to dig it out. Progress was slow and deliberate. He knew if he miscalculated, large stones above could be dislodged and thicken the wall. Hours went by and Janus was able to put only a few small stones behind him but he didn't stop. His life depended on making an air hole. He dug on.

Ten hours dragged by. Janus doggedly continued his task. The stone he was working on was the size of a closed fist. He felt it move slightly and he dug around the edges with his fingers. He gently tugged. This time the stone slowly gave up its place in the wall. Janus expected to see only blackness behind but instead a solitary distant star twinkled in a clear sky. Janus shuddered and took a deep breath. He would not die from lack of oxygen.

Janus continued to try, yet he was not able to free another stone or enlarge the hole. He watched Adamas' three moons pass in their orbit. He knew in a few hours it would be morning and wondered if anyone would return to look for him. As the sun's first rays began to lighten the sky, Janus heard faint voices. The sounds were weak and seemed far away. He shouted several times but his voice was muffled and only echoed in his dungeon.

An hour later the sun shone brightly. The voices remained distant. "How can I attract their attention?" Janus wondered. "No one can hear my shouting. What else is there? Yes! Maybe?" he thought. "The crystal that drew me to this spot." Finding the jagged stone in his basket, he raised his arm and worked his hand through the small opening. He slowly turned his hand so the crystal would reflect the sun's rays. He had no idea whether anyone could or would see the refracted light but this was his only hope.

For a long time nothing changed. Janus kept turning the crystal in his hand—silently he waited, praying someone would notice the flashes of light.

The previous afternoon, Sulia, Loria and Torak had searched for Janus after the avalanche until dark. They then camped beside the volcano. Many people had to return home to their families but promised to return with the sun. And they did return, bringing many more volunteers. Hundreds of people swarmed over the designated area where yesterday everyone had gathered crystals. They shouted, "Janus, Janus!!!" By noon, no one had found a sign of him but all kept looking.

After searching five hours, Sulia, Loria and Torak gathered for a rest on top of a boulder. Torak spoke glumly. "I can think of only two possibilites. I don't like either. One, Janus fell somewhere in this area and is hurt and unable to call or, two, he wandered outside of the climbing boundaries and was caught in the avalanche and probably killed. I think we should search either side of the red flags. There is always a chance. A storm is moving in and we won't have sun much longer."

Sulia looked worried but determined. She said she would start moving to the right. Torak and Loria went to the left. They agreed to whistle if they found anything.

Thirty minutes passed. Sulia slowly climbed and shouted. Intermittently tears filled her eyes and she had to stop and dry them. She looked up. A flash of white light caught her eyes. It disappeared and then came again. "Strange reflected light is always steady unless…" Sulia began to climb faster toward the flashing light.

"Janus, Janus, Janus!!" were the first words Janus heard. It was Sulia's voice. "Here, I'm here," he shouted. "Sulia, I'm here!"

Moments later he felt Sulia's hands cover his. Shaking with emotion, Janus spoke, "Please take your crystal, Sulia, I'm fine." Janus opened his hand.

Sulia grasped the crystal and Janus lowered his hand. Sulia peered into the small hole, laughing and crying as happy tears rolled down her cheeks. All she could say was, "Hi." Then she whistled and shouted for Torak and Loria.

In less than five minutes Torak, Loria and many others were beside Sulia carefully extracting the smaller stones and boulders that entombed Janus. Strong poles were brought to the spot. Master stonecutters indicated the large boulders to lever away without causing another slide or a cave in. Janus moved as far away as possible from the rapidly expanding opening. Soon the hole was large enough for Janus to pass his packbasket to waiting hands. Moments later Torak's strong arms pulled Janus up and out. It was a joyous reunion with lots of hugs, cheers and tears. The return to the village was a dancing, singing parade. Hearing the commotion, hundreds of people came out of their houses to join in the celebration.

That night in each house in the village, the families toasted Janus' return. In Torak and Loria's home a very special dinner was prepared by Loria, her mother and Sulia. The children insisted Janus tell them exactly what happened. And he did. Sealia, Robak and Starak leaned against Puss who was fast asleep.

"First of all," Janus began. "I made a big mistake. I did not pay attention or fully follow the master stonecutters' directions. This could have cost me my life and possibly others, too." Word-by-word he related the events of the two days. When he had finished, the children hugged him and ran to hug their parents and Sulia.

Janus and his adopted family then happily ate the magnificent dinner. When they had finished, Janus asked if he could be excused as he wanted to go to each house and thank everyone who had helped search for him or hoped for his safe return. He also wanted to apologize to the master stonecutters, who included Sulia's father. Loria and Torak agreed with his plan. Then Janus and Sulia kissed everyone good-night before they left to call on the villagers.

CHAPTER IV

Janus' remaining days passed too quickly. The thought that he must report to the rulers of Sagateum in a matter of hours weighed heavily on his mind.

During his last morning Janus worked in the garden with his family as usual. For the first time in memory everyone did his part in silence. It was a beautiful day, yet they knew that its was Janus' final day. Even Loopi and Puss sensed that something was wrong as they shadowed Janus and the children.

After a quiet lunch, Janus told Torak and Loria he needed to be alone. They understood.

Leaving the house, he set a course through Torak's orchard to a hill which overlooked the village. He found a shade tree and sat down to think.

Before he arrived on Adamas, Janus' mind had simply memorized the Elite's teachings. He was not supposed to think or question orders. Galactic pilots were trained to follow instructions. Tomorrow he was to transmit his findings to his mothership. Today he must make a decision—a very hard one.

Adamas had changed Janus forever. He knew he was a complete human with deep emotions and a creative mind. For the first time in his life he was a member of a family— a large family which extended beyond Torak's kin. Neighbors and friends had risked their lives to save his and Sulia would always be someone very special. Life had meaning on Adamas and life, Janus realized, was indeed precious.

Janus desperately searched his mind for a solution that would allow him to remain with people he loved. Each tentative idea was rejected by his knowledge of the Elite's sensitive technology which could detect the slightest falsehood in a space pilot's voice or radio wave signals. A failure to transmit at the appointed time would trigger the launching of a large heavily armed space vehicle from the mothership to investigate Adamas.

If he remained to defend Adamas, his small spacecraft would be wiped out in seconds by the military spacecraft. Adamas would gain merely a few moments of additional freedom before being slaughtered, enslaved and exploited. After two hours of mental anguish, Janus concluded that only if he transmitted the truth would the Elite on board the mothership believe his words.

There was no other choice. The only idea with any possibility of success was the worst possible solution. Janus could think of no other plan which would give Adamians a chance to live in peace. He hoped his gift to this gentle race of people would not be in vain and would fool the Elite.

The decision made, Janus gazed for a long time at the village below. He thought of the Adamians he loved and who waited for his return. He vowed his last night would be a joyous one.

Several miles away, Orrorak summoned the Council of the Chosen to an unprecedented meeting in his home. Fifty people gathered from nearby villages. Loria, Sulia and Torak were there.

"It is with a heavy heart that I have asked you here this afternoon for your advice," Orrorak began. "You are aware that recently an alien by the name of Janus landed on our planet. Tomorrow, he must communicate with his superiors and will probably leave. Janus described his planet as over-populated and depleted of natural resources. As an individual he is courageous, kind and intelligent; however, he has not told us the specific purpose of his visit or the policy of Sagateum's leaders regarding populated planets. Will his message to Sagateum's Elite jeopardize the future of every Adamian and the very existence of our planet? What do we do about Janus?"

For several minutes not one person moved. The impact of Orrorak's words fell heavily on each member of the Council.

Individuals silently pondered the possibilities that came to mind. No one enjoyed what he or she thought.

Finally several hands were raised. Orrorak nodded recognizing a member. "Yes, Doria?"

A handsome woman with gray hair stood. "Although I met Janus for only a few minutes when he visited our building, I liked him. I think we all do. In talking with him, I felt he was not only interested in what I was doing but wanted to know about me as a person. I know he likes Adamians, our values and our way of life. We have never intentionally hurt another human. I do not think we should start now. My suggestion, if it is necessary, is to destroy his spaceship."

Orrorak sat holding his chin in his hand and thanked Doria when she had finished. "That certainly is possible," he commented nodding toward Torak.

"I'm afraid our options are limited and may make no difference. If Janus does not communicate with his superiors, they will probably send out additional spaceships to investigate. They know he landed on our planet. According to Janus, it took approximately five of our years for him to reach Adamas. We could expect additional spaceships in that time or sooner."

"Assuming Janus transmits a full description of Adamas and the rulers of Sagateum are aggressive and covet the natural resources of our small planet, we can count on an invasion. Of course, we will do everything possible to defend ourselves. On the other hand, if Sagateum's leaders do not believe in taking over a populated planet, then we will be allowed to live in peace. I'm afraid the first of the two possibilites is more likely. Our family loves Janus very much and we believe he feels the same about us," Torak concluded. "We will miss him very much."

Orrorak sighed, "My friends, sadly I agree with Torak. Does anyone else have any other thoughts or ideas?" No one spoke. Orrorak continued, "We cannot change tomorrow nor fear the future. We will prepare as best we can for any eventuality but our ultimate fate may be in the hands of Janus."

Janus' last evening was as happy as possible. Before dinner he went for a walk with the children and their pets. Loria and Sulia made the dining room festive with glittering crystals and candles. During the meal everyone kept the conversation light. After the family had finished eating, neighbors began dropping in to wish Janus a safe journey. Each person said he or she would be happier if Janus stayed and became an Adamian. Janus thanked them all and told everyone that he would love to stay but felt he must go.

When it was time to say good-night, Janus felt it was better if final good-bys were said. He would get up at dawn and leave before breakfast. Sulia and Loria prepared a basket of food for him. Then it was time. There were lots of hugs and tears before everyone went to bed. No one slept.

Janus lay on his bed wide awake. Having made his decision, he was at peace. He knew what he planned to do was for the best. The hours passed slowly but finally a hint of dawn appeared. Janus rose, dressed, washed, hefted his backpack and left his home without daring to look back.

Above the fields, Janus crossed peaceful meadows. He appeared to be looking for something. Finally, he turned towards a large bush with bright red leaves and white berries. He picked one berry and put it in a pocket. Leaving the meadow behind, Janus continued the climb to his spaceship.

It looked exactly as he had left it. He pressed a button on his sleeve and stairs slowly descended. Janus reached in his pocket, took out the white berry, looked at it for just a moment and swallowed it. He hurried up the stairs, almost instantly feeling nauseous. Reaching the flight deck, he flipped switches as fast as possible. Suddenly he felt tired and very ill. All the spaceship systems were functioning and he pressed the transmission button. Then doubled up with pain, Janus spoke.

"This is Janus 777—in solar system 600,555 Planet III. Planet very small, has limited resources and toxic plants. Do not recommend further exploration. I am very sick and may die, but will attempt to return to mothership. End trans...."

Janus slumped over the console. He had done his best. The words he had spoken were true. Hopefully, the Elite would believe his message and Adamas would be spared. Now stomach cramps came in waves. He should take off but he wanted one more breath of fresh air and one last look at a world that could have been his home. Fighting the pain and sickness, Janus inched his way to the opening and clung onto the railing as he stumbled down the stairs. At the bottom he collapsed on the ground.

Torak, Loria and Sulia burst through the tree line running as fast as they could. They had come, at least, to wave good-by. When they saw Janus emerge from the spaceship and tumble down the stairs, they knew something was terribly wrong.

Torak first reached Janus.

"Janus!" Torak cried, "What is the matter?"

Janus looked up and even with the pain smiled broadly as Sulia and Loria arrived and fell to their knees beside him.

Sulia spoke sharply, "Janus, what did you do? Tell me!"

Janus lowered his eyes and whispered, "White berry," as his head rolled to the side.

Loria screamed, "No, no!"

"How many did you eat?" Sulia demanded. "Answer me, Janus!"

Janus raised one finger.

Sulia immediately opened her small hip pack. She always carried an antidote for the white berry. Most adults did.

Sulia murmured, "It may not be too late if Janus doesn't lose consciousness. Hold his head up while I pour this liquid into his mouth. Open your mouth Janus, please, please...."

His eyes remained closed, but Janus followed directions and human reflexes did the rest. He swallowed as Sulia poured half the bottle down his throat. She turned to Loria and Torak, "Now we must get him up and walking and keep him awake."

Torak grabbed one of Janus' arms and pulled him to his feet. Sulia held the other. They began walking continually talking to him. Janus' head had fallen to his chest. He only mumbled. Round and round they walked.

Janus began to gag, then bent over and threw up. Sulia smiled and told Janus to drink again. His head now level, Janus opened his mouth without further prompting and swallowed. They resumed walking. Sulia knew Janus was past the crisis. He would live. The antidote had worked. Finally, Janus spoke clearly. "I think we can stop and sit down. The pains have gone away. I feel weak but no longer nauseous."

As soon as they were seated in the shade of the spaceship, Loria simply asked, "Why, Janus?"

Janus quietly described the mission of all galactic pilots and the demands of the Elite on his planet. "I thought what I did would give Adamas a chance to survive. Sadly, I still must go. The Monitors on the mothership will be suspicious when my message reaches them and there is no indication I took off. So I must leave immediately."

"Listen, Janus," insisted Torak, "tell me if I am wrong. Your spaceship has automatic pilot and you can program it to follow any set of coordinates in the universe. You can even program the ship·so it will blow up or launch itself. Is that correct?"

With a hint of a knowing smile, Janus nodded.

"My suggestion," Torak continued, "is that you program your spaceship to take off. Set the coordinates to your mothership but make one small error so that your spaceship will fly directly into a star. Lock the program in so the Monitors will not be able to override your commands. By the time they receive the flight data, they will assume your mistake was due to your sickness. You died from the poison or from your spaceship crashing into a sun. Hopefully, the Elite of Sagateum will decide further exploration of our solar system is not worthwhile."

An Adamian had amazed Janus again. "I don't know how you know so much, Torak," Janus grinned. "Of course, you're right! Let's do it. Care to watch? Come on!"

Janus climbed up the stairway with the threesome right behind him. While Loria, Sulia and Torak explored the interior, Janus began adjusting computers and entering data. It wasn't long before he called, "Time to say good-by." And this time Janus was smiling as they descended the ladder. Janus pushed the button on his sleeve again and the accordion stairs retracted. Quickly, the group moved away, held hands and waited. Soon the spaceship came to life. It began to hover as the landing pods were withdrawn inside the ship. The craft began a slow rotation rising higher and higher.

"Once above your gravity field, the spaceship will go timespeed," explained Janus.

"Not quite correct, Janus," Loria added with a wink. She looked at Janus like a long lost brother. "Now it is OUR gravity field." Everyone laughed.

Janus smiled, "Right, Loria. If you will have me, I would be proud to be considered an Adamian." Then his face turned serious, "Sulia, how can I ever begin to repay you? You saved my life twice. Words will never be enough. What a debt!"

Sulia squeezed Janus' hand. With a twinkle in her eye and a loving smile she replied, "Don't worry, Janus; give me time and I will think of something." They all laughed again. Janus' space craft was barely visible when they turned for home.

CHAPTER V

By the time they reached the village, everyone knew Janus had returned to stay.

During dinner Torak mentioned he had received word that Orrorak would like Janus to visit the Crystal Palace. The adults stayed up late talking. Janus wondered out loud how he could help Adamians. Life was so wonderfully different here.

Torak chuckled, "Don't worry, Janus. Orrorak will find something for you to do. We may not be quite so different as you think. Tomorrow I work at the Crystal Palace. We will go together."

Sulia and Loria smiled but wouldn't expand upon Torak's answer except to say "tomorrow."

Torak and Janus rose early, ate a quick breakfast and hurried through the village as the faint rays of dawn silhouetted men and women heading in all directions. They joined those walking toward Lake Jennifer.

As the two friends walked, Janus asked many questions. Those that pertained to the Crystal Palace Torak answered by repeating "Orrorak will explain." He did admit going out there often to study but wouldn't say more. Within an hour they came to the shores of beautiful Lake Jennifer. It was a gigantic lake and a busy one. Even in the early morning haze one could see hundreds of sailing crafts docking and departing from a long stone pier. Some were fishing boats whereas others carried passengers.

"This way," called Torak, as he stepped aboard one of the boats. "We're lucky today. The wind is blowing toward the island. Some days we get our early morning exercise by using the oars and rowing. In the evening sail boats often have to tack, providing a leisurely return. Individuals who want to work up an appetite select a rowing or poling boat."

Janus listened as Torak described the lake in detail but they were interrupted often by their fellow passengers who introduced themselves and shook hands. As the fog began to thin, Janus could just make out the outline of a large island. The strong breeze pushed them faster. With land near, just like a curtain in a theater going up, the haze lifted and the Crystal Palace sparkled in the sunlight. Janus thought it the most beautiful building he had ever seen.

Hordes of people were streaming up the towering marble steps which led to the high entrance. Torak pointed out Orrorak standing at the top. Each person seemed to pause, shake hands with him, say a few words and then go on.

"Welcome, Janus, welcome!" Orrorak said shaking Janus' hands and hugging him and then Torak. The three men spoke briefly before Torak excused himself.

"Janus," Torak called back, "I know you will have a very interesting day with our number one guide." Orrorak smiled.

Orrorak led Janus through the entrance, stopped and placed his hands on Janus' shoulders.

"Janus," Orrorak began, "I speak for all Adamians. What you did yesterday will never be forgotten. The sacrifice you were willing to make to protect our planet was the ultimate gift of love. We are honored that you are now an Adamian."

Orrorak did not try to stop the tear that trickled down his cheek. It took a few moments before he could continue.

"We won't be able to see everything today but we hope you will want to spend part of your life here at the Crystal Palace."

They turned the corner. In front of them was a huge room. In the center was a raised circular stage with computers. In front of each computer sat students receiving guidance from older men and women. On the walls large television and holographic screens flashed with numbers, pictures, shapes, equations and three-dimensional people speaking.

Janus' eyes opened wide but nothing came from his lips.

Like a teacher with a new student, Orrorak continued the story. "Across the corridor are some of our laboratories. Let's take a look."

Orrorak took a few steps and opened a door. "This is one of our land science labs."

Janus stared at a modern laboratory that seemed to go on and on. Women and men were bent over advanced microscopes, computers and complex electronic equipment. There were cages with animals of various sizes, aquariums full of marine life and hundreds of glass containers with various species of plants. On shelves, labeled plastic boxes held different minerals and jars contained colored liquids.

"This is Sulia's domain and part of her responsibilities. People here study the few diseases on our planet, herbal medicines, chemistry, mineralogy, genetic engineering and related disciplines."

"Now," Orrorak announced with a smile, "let's go see what is happening in the area I call fun and games." Janus could barely return Orrorak's smile. His head was swimming.

They crossed to a mammoth building and took a silent elevator which opened to a catwalk high above another world. Janus gazed in amazement. Below him, men and women were testing a jet helicopter, a land vehicle, laser weapons and inside the open dome, Janus saw a gigantic, hovering radio telescope. In the distance a huge spaceship was being constructed. Robots scurried here and there helping. A young woman with a flight power pack waved as she flew by.

"We hope you might like to work with our engineers," Orrorak explained. "They invent all sorts of products and we have the capability to test each one fully but rarely do we make more than a prototype. For example, here is an interesting gadget. Like most of our inventions, it is one of a kind and no more will be built. Janus, put these earphones on and I will put a set on, too."

"Listen. What do you hear?" asked Orrorak. Janus heard a non-human voice, "Janus is wondering how we have created this technology."

Orrorak spoke, "Janus, that was my thought you just heard. And you were thinking, this device may be some sort of cassette recorder." Orrorak smiled as Janus shook his head in awe. Orrorak continued, "Yes, this instrument transmits other people's thoughts. It will never be used on Adamas."

Slowly they wandered back towards the front of the Palace.

Orrorak picked up two pieces of fruit. Eating in silence, they moved along. Finally, Orrorak stopped in front of a set of double doors. Above the entrance there was a simple sign with large gold letters: Hall of Honor. Janus and Orrorak entered a magnificent auditorium.

Janus was astounded. He couldn't believe what he had seen. Adamas possessed technology that equaled or even surpassed Sagateum's. Why did these people live so simply? Why do physical labor when robots could do the work? Why?

"Janus, please sit down," the old man said. "You are surprised at what you have seen and can't understand our way of life. Maybe if I tell you how this all came to pass, you won't think we are quite so crazy."

Janus nodded and smiled in awe as he stared at the beautiful mural in front of him. Faces of a different species of human beings looked down upon him. In the picture was a large spaceship with the word *Democritus* painted on its side.

Orrorak spoke softly, "Over 100 years ago a spaceship from a planet called Earth landed with difficulty on Adamas. The ten astronauts on board were friendly and proved to be very kind. In time we learned they and their superiors did not believe Earthlings should invade a planet populated with intelligent forms of life. They believed amongst the 100 billion stars in their own Milky Way galaxy and the 100 billion galaxies of the universe that their astronauts would find uninhabited planets to colonize.

"For weeks the astronauts tried to repair their spaceship and communicate with their mothership stationed several galaxies away. They were unsuccessful on both counts and asked if they could live on Adamas.

"We were astonished. They asked us! We believed they were almost gods. Why should they ask for anything? They possessed knowledge far beyond our comprehension. They had instant fire, laser weapons like your pistol, power packs which allowed them to fly like birds, food that required only water to become delicious and much, much, more. A language analyzer, similar to yours, allowed them to learn our language overnight; yet, each astronaut took pains to learn our customs and study our way of life. We quickly realized these powerful people meant us no harm. They could easily have become the rulers of the planet. Instead, they became our dearest friends.

"Although I was quite young, I was chosen to ask their leader for a meeting. He had a funny name, George. He agreed but suggested each village on Adamas send the most admired woman and man to the meeting. This group became the first Council of the Chosen.

"We gathered on this sacred island and sat in a large circle underneath our ancient Biraak trees. I was afraid and shy, but had been asked to speak. 'George, I began, will you and your friends share your knowledge so Adamians may have the things and capabilities you have?' I quickly sat down.

"George stood and spoke in a quiet voice, 'Since we landed on your beautiful planet, Adamians have made us feel welcome, given us food and lodging and trusted us with their very lives. Of course, my friends, we will be happy to share our knowledge but first let me ask you a question. What do you value most in your society here on Adamas? Please let us hear from all of you.'

"Silence. Finally a small woman of a good many years spoke. 'The joy of my life is working in our garden with my husband—a husband who likes to sing, loves his children and is my best friend.' The old woman turned to look at a gray haired man sitting beside her who grinned. Many of us laughed but George and his friends just smiled and nodded.

"Others spoke, 'Well sewn clothes,' 'Close friends,' 'Talented artisans and honest people,' 'Singers and dancers,' 'Generous and friendly neighbors,' 'Artists that amaze us with their creations and actors who capture our imagination.' And finally, I added, 'Our freedom, independence and ancestors who taught us to love and care for all we have on Adamas.'

"George returned to his feet, 'My friends, we earthlings over centuries created a highly technical society and in many ways a wonderful world. However, not all our inventions meant a better life for all. In some ways we may not have been as wise as you. We invented products and created sophisticated technology without thinking or evaluating their long-term effects on people and our planet. We talked little about what progress truly is. Our world contains many races, religions and cultures and it took us thousands of years to learn to live in peace. We found it difficult to control our economies, population growth and pollution and to wisely conserve and share our natural resources. If you wish to learn our technical knowledge, then I ask that we discuss what kind of progress you really want for Adamas.'"

Orrorak continued, "Adamian philosophy includes the idea that time is a gentle friend so George's request seemed reasonable. I suggested we return to our villages to discuss George's proposal. If our neighbors and friends agreed, we would construct a special building on this island for our meetings with the astronauts. The Council agreed and we departed. Weeks later we returned with thousands of volunteers and master stone builders. The designers created a building that could grow. When we had completed one large room, the meetings with the earthlings began.

"George opened the first meeting by asking what we wanted progress to do for us.

"It wasn't an easy question to answer. No, we didn't want life easier. We knew the physical work in our gardens was good for us and we enjoyed it. It gave us feelings of accomplishment, personal independence and a knowledge and reverence for life. And, of course, it earned the respect of our neighbors and friends.

"A young woman stood and asked if progress would encourage us to become more sensitive to the feelings of others? Could it help us better care for everything in our world and teach us to wisely preserve all the good things we have? Would the knowledge Earthlings possessed allow Adamians to understand more about themselves and others and maybe even people on distant planets?

"All the astronauts applauded. Lia sat down.

"An astronaut by the name of Jennifer smiled and rose to speak. 'Lia, if this Council and the neighbors you represent will always judge progress on the basis of your questions, I know we will always be happy help to you.'

"Then Jennifer continued, 'Permit us to assist your master stone builders in creating other rooms so we may bring the instruments, machines and computers from our spaceship to the Crystal Palace. We will share with you the knowledge of our planet and what limited wisdom we possess. The Council of the Chosen must pass judgement on whether or not specific knowledge would mean progress for all who live on Adamas.'

"Many months later the astronauts' spaceship had been dismantled and their equipment installed in the Crystal Palace. They brought with them vast amounts of knowledge on microchips. We began studying their people's discoveries and inventions. All their computers were solar-powered as is every moving thing you saw today.

"The Council of the Chosen met daily to discuss what we were learning. Sometimes we spent days talking about the early earthlings inventions. The wheel was the first item the Council agreed would be good to introduce in our society. We believed it would not change the basic values of our way of life. So today Janus, you see small carts and wagons wherever you go."

Janus commented, "I understand so far but a few minutes ago I saw an advanced land vehicle. Why don't you make cars and trucks?"

"Oh," Orrorak continued, "we talked a long time about powered vehicles. Even today engineers like to tinker with our prototype vehicle, testing it on our computers, but the Council, our neighbors and engineers agreed that rushing somewhere has never been important in Adamian philosophy. Jogging is good exercise. Thousands of people volunteer and relays of messengers take letters to any corner of our planet in days. In an emergency our laser communication system links every village in seconds. Fortunately, we have only had to test the system.

"Now the printing press is another story. You visited the village's printing press which is used to make books. On earth it is very outdated but on our planet we believe it is just about right. It takes time and care to create, print and bind a single book. The resources of our planet that are used to make a book are valuable to everyone. Each book is precious, respected and shared by all.

"Thanks to the astronauts' microchips, people of all ages come to the Crystal Palace to read the greatest literature the planet earth produced. Adamians don't need to wait until we print a book. We are developing some fine writers and many of their works are now books.

"In our laboratories you saw plants which are studied for many reasons. This is equally true regarding technology. Recently, we discovered light can be used as a power source for spaceships and as a powerful weapon. This knowledge will allow us to visit planets outside our solar system as well as to protect Adamas. But more important than space flights is the return of our explorers to a beautiful world. A planet which, after thousands of years of human habitation, remains rich in natural resources and a joy for its people.

"Every invention is discussed a long time before we even make a prototype. Our astronaut friends emphasized technology would have long-term effects. They related sad stories of chemicals and inventions that were created to improve life on Earth and didn't. We continue to debate television. Adamians believe sports, hiking and climbing are healthier for the body and mind than sitting and watching someone on a T.V. screen. Every village has its own live theater and places for people to study other creative arts. For now, television is just one facet of our education and the communication system here at the Crystal Palace.

"The Earthlings lived long and happy lives on Adamas. They married, had children and became Adamians. If George were living today, he would be proud of his great, great granddaughter Sulia. Janus, does our philosophy of life and concept of progress make any sense to you?"

Janus was overwhelmed by the depth of these people. "Yes," was all he could say.

Orrorak took Janus' hands. "We choose to live simply but we are no longer a simple people. You are now an Adamian and we want you to be a member of the Council of the Chosen. We hope you will live a long and happy life with us. Some day you may fall in love, marry and have children."

Janus looked directly into the eyes of the old man. "This man is the father I never had," he thought.

Janus spoke, "Orrorak, you and many Adamians have taught me so much and have given me the chance to truly live. I never knew what it meant to have a family, be happy or feel grateful." Janus paused and grinned. "I hope somewhere on Adamas there is a woman who will one day be my wife."

Orrorak winked and had the last word, "Janus, my young friend, I think you can count on it."

They both laughed, rose and left the Hall of Honor.

Outside, they paused to absorb the view. Their planet's beauty and serenity lay before them. An aura of love and peace, like rays from a sun, rose from the lake below, from the peopled green valleys, the distant effervescent mountains and even

from the far off great blue waters. Side-by-side, Janus and Orrorak took their first steps together and began to slowly walk down the thousand iridescent steps of the Crystal Palace of Adamas.